I KNOW WHAT TO DO! SOCIAL SKILLS

HOW TO IDENTIFY YOUR EMOTIONS

CAITIE MCANENEY

PowerKiDS press

Published in 2025 by The Rosen Publishing Group, Inc.
2544 Clinton Street, Buffalo, NY 14224

First Edition

Editor: Caitie McAneney
Book Design: Rachel Rising

Photo Credits: Cover, p. 1 unguryanu/Shutterstock.com; pp. 4, 6, 8, 10, 12, 14, 16, 18, 20, 21 Cute art/Shutterstock.com; p. 5 LAONG/Shutterstock.com; p. 7 DesignerThce/Shutterstock.com; p. 9 Pixel-Shot/ Shutterstock.com; p. 11 Prostock-studio/Shutterstock.com; p. 13 ESB Professional/Shutterstock.com; p. 15 SE Arts Media/Shutterstock.com; p. 17 vectorfusionart/Shutterstock.com; p. 19 onstockphoto/Shutterstock.com; p. 21 Evgeny Atamanenko/Shutterstock.com.

Library of Congress Cataloging-in-Publication Data

Names: McAneney, Caitie, author.
Title: How to identify your emotions / Caitie McAneney.
Description: Buffalo, NY : PowerKids Press, [2025] | Series: I know what to do! social skills | Includes index.
Identifiers: LCCN 2024031193 (print) | LCCN 2024031194 (ebook) | ISBN 9781499450514 (library binding) | ISBN 9781499450507 (paperback) | ISBN 9781499450521 (ebook)
Subjects: LCSH: Emotions–Juvenile literature. | Social skills–Study and teaching–Juvenile literature.
Classification: LCC BF531 .M329 2025 (print) | LCC BF531 (ebook) | DDC 152.4–dc23/eng/20240710
LC record available at https://lccn.loc.gov/2024031193
LC ebook record available at https://lccn.loc.gov/2024031194

Manufactured in the United States of America

CPSIA Compliance Information: Batch #CWPK25. For Further Information contact Rosen Publishing at 1-800-237-9932

CONTENTS

What Are Emotions?

What do you feel right now? Maybe you have a big feeling. Maybe you feel "okay." Whatever you're feeling, that's your emotion. Emotions are important. They are not good or bad. Emotions help you **experience** the world. They let you know what's right for you.

Getting Curious

It can be hard to name emotions. You may just feel "bad" or "upset." You may feel "**neutral**." Get curious. You can look at a feelings wheel or list. What emotion seems true to you? You may think you're mad. You may actually be **frustrated**.

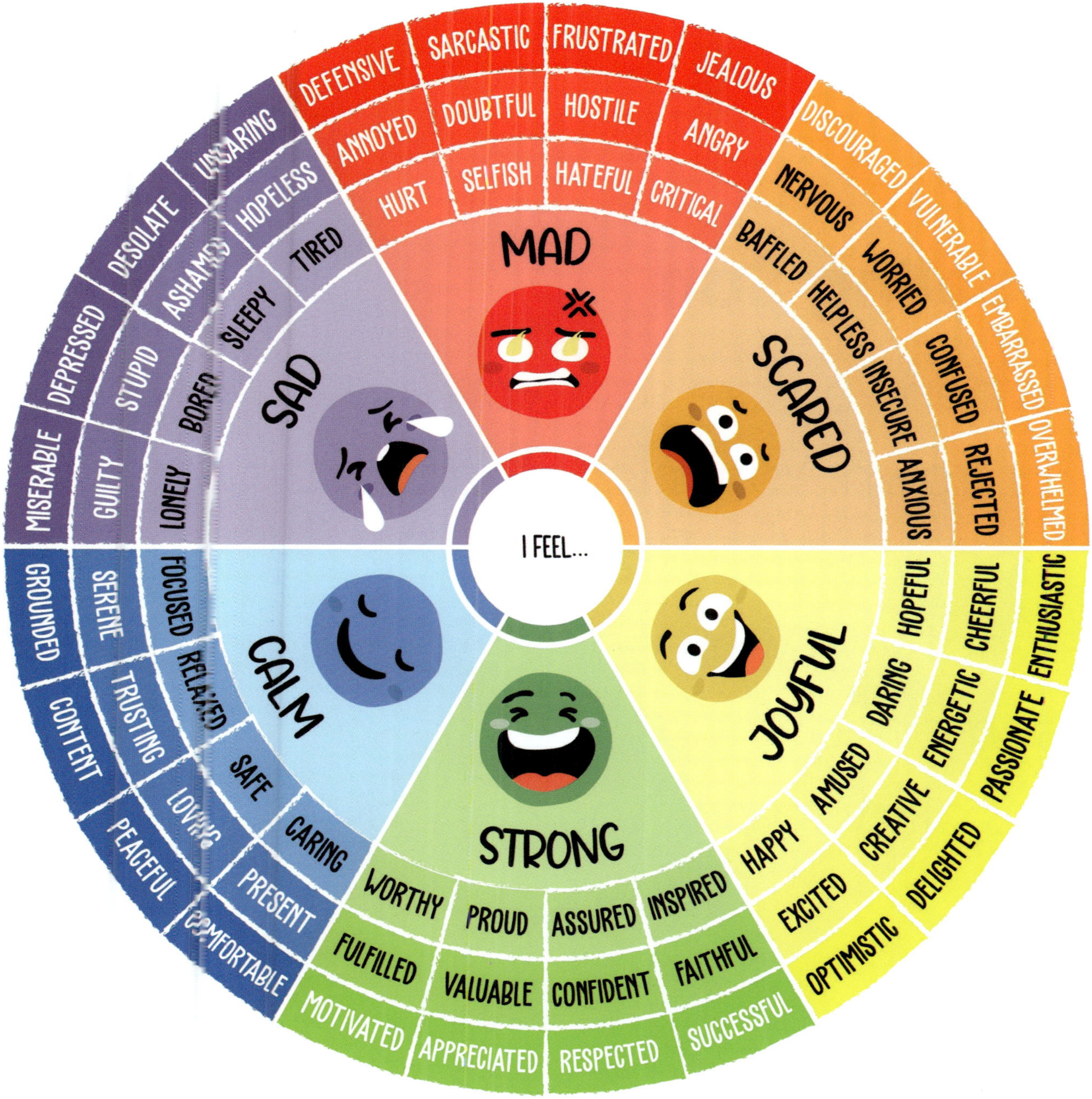
I FEEL...
MAD
HURT
SELFISH
HATEFUL
CRITICAL
ANNOYED
DOUBTFUL
HOSTILE
ANGRY
DEFENSIVE
SARCASTIC
FRUSTRATED
JEALOUS
SCARED
BAFFLED
HELPLESS
INSECURE
ANXIOUS
NERVOUS
WORRIED
CONFUSED
REJECTED
DISCOURAGED
VULNERABLE
EMBARRASSED
OVERWHELMED
JOYFUL
HOPEFUL
DARING
AMUSED
HAPPY
CHEERFUL
ENERGETIC
CREATIVE
EXCITED
ENTHUSIASTIC
PASSIONATE
DELIGHTED
OPTIMISTIC
STRONG
WORTHY
PROUD
ASSURED
INSPIRED
FULFILLED
VALUABLE
CONFIDENT
FAITHFUL
MOTIVATED
APPRECIATED
RESPECTED
SUCCESSFUL
CALM
FOCUSED
RELAXED
SAFE
CARING
SERENE
TRUSTING
LOVING
PRESENT
GROUNDED
CONTENT
PEACEFUL
COMFORTABLE
SAD
TIRED
SLEEPY
BORED
LONELY
HOPELESS
ASHAMED
STUPID
GUILTY
UNCARING
DESOLATE
DEPRESSED
MISERABLE

Feeling Sad

When you are sad, you may cry or frown. You might feel low or hopeless. Maybe you didn't get what you wanted. Maybe you miss someone. It's okay to be sad. It's okay to cry. You can talk it out.

Feeling Mad

When you are mad, your face might turn red. You might feel warm and **tense**. What's behind that anger? Maybe you are frustrated or **jealous**. You might be hurt or bothered. It's okay. You can work through it. Tell someone you trust.

Feeling Excited

When you are excited, you may have a lot of energy. You might be looking forward to something. Maybe you can't wait for your birthday or a field trip. Looking forward to something is also called anticipation. What makes you feel excited?

Feeling Scared

When you feel scared, you may want to run or hide. You might be afraid something bad will happen. You might feel anxious, or worried about something. It may help to talk about your fears. Things will feel less scary after.

Feeling Happy

When you feel happy, you may feel silly and joyful. It may be hard to sit still! You may be happy when you're with someone you love. You may be happy when you're doing your favorite thing, like dancing. What makes you happy?

The Body Knows

Your body gives you clues to your emotions. If you feel heavy and tired, you may be sad. If you feel tense in your face, you may be mad. If you shake or shrink, you may be scared. Feeling worried can make your stomach hurt.

Dealing with Feelings

It's normal to have emotions. They come and go. **Identifying** the emotion is the first step. Next, you can take time to breathe. Then, you can talk about your emotion. There is no shame in feeling things. Once you feel, you can heal.

PRACTICE MAKES PROGRESS!

To talk about feelings, you can say:

"When that happened, I felt sad."

"I need a minute to calm down."

"I'm upset and I need help."

"I feel mad at my friend. What can I do?"

GLOSSARY

experience: Something that a person has done or lived through.

frustrated: Feeling upset or angry because of being unable to do what one needs to do or solve a problem.

identify: To find out or show what something is.

jealous: Feeling angry or sad when you want what another person has.

neutral: Not one thing or another.

tense: Feeling strained or tight in body or mind.

FOR MORE INFORMATION

BOOKS

Chang, Kirsten. *Scared*. Minneapolis, MN: Bellwether Media, Inc., 2025.

Woolley, Katie. *Mental Well-Being and Mindfulness*. Buffalo, NY: PowerKids Press, 2024.

WEBSITES

Feelings Games
pbskids.org/games/feelings
Have fun with feelings! Discover new games about feelings with PBS Kids.

What to Do When You Feel Sad
kidshealth.org/en/kids/depression.html#catemotion
Explore tips for coping with big feelings.

Publisher's note to educators and parents: Our editors have carefully reviewed these websites to ensure that they are suitable for students. Many websites change frequently, however, and we cannot guarantee that a site's future contents will continue to meet our high standards of quality and educational value. Be advised that students should be closely supervised whenever they access the internet.

INDEX